THE OIL CREEK CHRONICLES

RICHARD W. AITES

iUniverse, Inc.
New York   Bloomington

THE OIL CREEK CHRONICLES

Copyright © 2009 by Richard W. Aites

Disclaimer: This is a work of fiction. All of the characters, names, incidents, organizations, and dialogue in this novel are either the products of the author's imagination or are used fictitiously.

iUniverse books may be ordered through booksellers or by contacting:

iUniverse
1663 Liberty Drive
Bloomington, IN 47403
www.iuniverse.com
1-800-Authors (1-800-288-4677)

ISBN: 978-1-4401-2801-1 (pbk)
ISBN: 978-1-4401-2802-8 (ebk)

Printed in the United States of America

iUniverse Rev. 3/17/09

AUTHOR'S NOTE:

The Residents of the Oil Region in northwestern, Pennsylvania who read this story will surely recognize some of the names, events and places. As noted by the Publisher of this work, this is a historical fiction piece and the persons described in thereof are used fictitiously. As with my first book 'The Legend of Coal Oil Johnny', the names of both people and places are used to help the reader appreciate their heritage and the history of the region. It is also a subtle way of expressing my gratitude to those wonderful people who versed me so well in the old myths and legends of the place. For those fabulous recollections that have helped make the history of the region so colorful, have also contributed greatly to this story. Unlike 'The Legend of Coal Oil Johnny', which was based on a real live character and factual history, the rising waters of 'The Oil Creek Chronicles' crashes through the valley corridor without such barriers or limitations. Like 'Coal Oil Johnny', the fictional narrator is the same.

And though this story is intended for all readers of all ages, my hope is that it brings some enjoyment to the wonderful people of my former hometowns of Rouseville and Oil City. I also hope that it will reach the younger generation of the region, to remind them of the wonderful natural resources that are available to them. Hunting, fishing and exploring are good for both the body and the soul. Nature certainly has a way of refreshing one's spirit.

PREFACE

The 1980's were a difficult time for many that resided in northwestern Pennsylvania. The closing of factories, mills and massive layoffs brought much hardship to the region. My family struggled mightily after my Father was laid off from a good paying job in Franklin, PA. We, like many, relied on government assistance for quite some time. Our situation was often so dire that a Samaritan and neighbor often left bags of food that he acquired from a local church pantry, at our front door to help feed me and my four siblings. I recall that my Mother was often depressed during the holidays because there wouldn't be much for her children at Christmas, but there was always the promise of next year.

I remember how delighted I was when that next Christmas came and I received a brand new fishing rod and a used Harrington & Richardson single-shot shotgun for my brothers and I to share. Times remained difficult but I believe that for my family and the thousands of others who had to struggle during those tough economic times, we were all the better for it. Enduring such hardship not only builds and strengthens one's character but it also leaves them with a greater appreciation of the finer things in life.

At 14 I was truly fortunate to have the opportunity to grasp the outdoors and to live and play in such a beautiful region of this Country, of which I write so much about. During my high school years I spent countless afternoons and evenings fishing Oil Creek and its tributaries and hunting and exploring the picturesque hills that enveloped the scenic little valley. I was also fortunate enough to have a good rapport with most of the people in town, and on those evenings when I wasn't in the woods taking potshots at squirrels or down at the creek landing a mess of trout, I was listening to the town's Elders reciting the old myths and legends of the place. Unlike most of my friends and siblings, I actually enjoyed the historic tales.

Rouseville was just one of many small towns in the region that still remained from the early Oil Boom days. And though most small towns across America have a story, a history, very few can boast of such a colorful and industrious past. The history of this region extends well back beyond the great boom of the 1860's and 1870's. Decades earlier skirmishes were fought between the local Native Americans and invading settlers. Before the settlers arrived, wolves, bears and panthers (mountain lions) roamed the heavily wooded hills while deer and elk browsed and grazed in the lush, green plateaus. Eventually the Indians (namely the Seneca) were forced out and the Oil Creek Valley was now the home of mostly Scots-Irish and German immigrants. These new citizens prospered but the wildlife suffered immensely when a government bounty helped eliminate the predators-especially wolves- and hunting for both sustenance and sport nearly wiped out all of the deer and other large game.

By the 1840's these same immigrants worked hard to forge farms from a rough, infertile land that only the hardiest of men and women could have conquered. So it is here, nearly a decade before Edwin Drake's famous oil well and the massive influx of humanity and greed that followed, where our story begins...

Chapter 1

As recited by Mr. Andrew Buchanan of Franklin, PA in 1923:

My Father was the beneficiary of a small parcel of land near the confluence of Oil Creek and Cherry Run. Jonathon Scot Buchanan had once resided on the acreage but had abandoned it a few years earlier when he rushed out west in the quest for gold. Unfortunately my Father's only sibling never found his fortune but instead contracted a fever and died shortly thereafter. Once word finally reached my Father of my Uncle's demise, he was stricken with grief and fell into a terrible bout of melancholy. Hardened by years of backbreaking labor in a sweltering blast furnace in Potter County, PA, my Father was much like the pig iron he used to help forge; it would bend but never break. Yet the loss of his brother appeared to be draining the life right out of him. My Mother became deeply concerned with his condition and visited the local Doctor in the hope of finding a cure. He suggested that my Father needed a change of scenery.

Before departing for California, my Uncle had made the journey from Oil Creek to our home in Coudersport to bid farewell. There was a sparkle about the young Irishman's eyes when he spoke about the fortune in gold he was sure to discover. Confident of his pending wealth, he promised my Father a portion of it and, a better life. My Father in return held back his sarcasm and was a lot less critical of Jonathon's spontaneous venture than one might have suspected. My Mother was the one that actually tried to convince him otherwise. She knew that the long journey across the continent could be a dangerous one. In those days St. Louis was still the westernmost edge of civilization and beyond that lurked hostile Indians, outlaws and bandits and extreme climates. My Uncle took her concerns in consideration, but only for the moment. My Mother who adored Uncle John nearly as much as my Father, cursed him for a fool and then hugged him tightly while tears rolled down across her flushed cheeks. On the day prior to his departure, he concocted a will that listed my Father as the only benefactor to everything he owned. He confided in my Father that he wasn't much of a farmer anyway, and relied heavily on the generous bounty of fish and game that flourished in the local streams and surrounding hills. He claimed that what little corn he did cultivate, was actually reserved for the distillation of whiskey.

So it was nearly two years to the day of my Uncle's departure when we received word that a bad case of scarlet fever had taken his life and his body had been laid to rest at a mining camp near San Francisco. My Mother had finally gotten up enough nerve to inform my Father about the Doctor's suggestion, and after a fit of hostility geared towards her so-called defiance, he calmed down and thought things over. At that time Potter County was becoming overpopulated, at least in my Father's mind, with Norwegian Settlers. The lumber industry and the cultivation of potatoes had brought much prosperity to the area but also attracted undesirables. Horse thievery and livestock rustling was all too common and there was very little law to protect those who needed it.

As my Father pondered over the Doctor's advice, a hard winter settled in. A thick carpet of snow blanketed the ground for several weeks and when the rivers iced over, commerce slowed and the iron furnaces closed down.

In March of 1853 the weather broke, therefore we loaded up our belongings and made the 160 mile trek to Cornplanter Township, in Venango County. Upon our arrival nearly two weeks later, I could see the subtle disappointment on my Mother's face.

Weeds as tall as a man, thick strands of poverty grass and the thorny tentacles of briar bushes enveloped the meager piece of land. The rustic looking log home was intact, but barely. The roof, which was fashioned of bark shingles, was in desperate need of repair. The mortar from the stone fireplace was crumbling and many of the floor boards needed to be replaced. To the rear of the cabin was a rickety, weathered fence that encompassed a half-acre plot of more weeds and briars. The decomposing shells of squash and other gourd vegetables laid strewn about the entangled mess.

Upon closer inspection of the property, our disappointment didn't last long.

The seven acres on which the farm rested was more than double the size of land we'd owned in Potter County. Though scrub timber and gray moss-covered boulders, some as large as a wagon, blotted the surrounding hillside, the neglected crop field was relatively clear. Still, much hard work would be required to get the farm ready for planting but my Father was a hardy man and hard work rarely discouraged this seemingly tireless soul.

I myself was very pleased with our relocation. Within a few days of our arrival I was allowed to explore the outer perimeter of our newly acquired property. It was of great surprise to find that our land was at the intersection of two fine trout streams. Oil Creek was the larger of the two, more a river than a creek, while Cherry Run was the swift little brook that spilled into the 'crick' at the westernmost end of the farm. Steep, wooded hills and thick, brushy plateaus surrounded us to the east and west. And

I would later learn of the closeness of proximity to several neighboring farms.

Years later I questioned my Mother in regards to my Father's decision in moving to his deceased brother's land. I figured that the memory of his beloved sibling would cause more grief and heartache, for I knew how much he missed his brother. She then reckoned that my Father needed to be closer to the spirit of his brother. She reasoned that the move helped fill the empty void that my Uncle's untimely death had created. Though my father would never admit it, my Mother was right. No amount of horse thievery or over-crowding of immigrants could have convinced his stubborn soul to make such a decisive move.

CHAPTER 2

The Oil Creek Valley turned out to be a majestic place, especially for a boy. The climate was temperate and comfortable. Even in the heat of summer the nights were so chilly that condensation saturated the ground and a thick layer of fog hovered above the valley floor. Once the yawning Sun rose above the steep hillsides late in the morning, the fog and dew would evaporate and the afternoon was relatively humidity free. Wild rose, jack-in-the-pulpit and day lilies thrived along the edges of our property, and the creek banks were thick with blackberry, elderberry and raspberry bushes. The constant, gentle breeze that permeated through the valley carried with it the fresh scent of honeysuckle, juniper, and mountain mint. Chestnut, butternut and hickory trees abounded in the woods beyond the farm and giant pin-oak and birch trees dominated the hillsides.

Shortly after the restoration of the farm and the planting of crops, my Father finally convinced my Mother that it was safe for me to get out and explore the surrounding countryside. He believed that once the chores were completed, it was good to get out and find recreation in nature. As a boy himself, growing up in Potter County, he spent much time fishing the river or exploring the big woods with Jonathon. Since arriving in the valley several weeks earlier, I had the terrible itch to do some fishing myself and was fortunate to be within a stones throw of two crystal clear streams. Jonathon had told my Father that the creeks were full of plump bass, tasty bream, and delicious speckled (brook) trout. My mouth was watering at the thought of fish for supper.

During short breaks from our hard work around the farm, my Father built me a fishing pole. The piece was crafted from the limb of a large, reed-like plant that grew on the hillside above our property. After several days of drying and a good coating of beeswax, which added some spring and durability, a tiny, iron eye-lit was fastened to the very tip. The reel was a wooden spool that was wrapped with several yards of fishing line that my Father had acquired during our trip. He also presented me with a handful of small hooks and some sinkers that were fashioned from lead buckshot. With my new cane pole in hand and a can of red worms that I had dug up in my Mother's new garden, I was headed for the creek.

It was during this time that I met a cherished, life-long friend in Johnny Steele.

While fishing that day Johnny saved my rump from an angry rattlesnake, which I would soon discover were common tenants along the creek. I would later follow Johnny to his home, the McClintock Farm, which was situated on the opposite side of Oil Creek about a half mile north of our place. The farm was several times larger than our own and contained two massive crop fields. Several head of livestock grazed about the property. I was then introduced to Johnny's foster- parents who were both very fine people. I learned that Johnny had lived on the McClintock farm since he was a toddler and that his interest in fishing and exploring was even greater than mine. My Parents were later introduced to the McClintocks and became good friends. We even became parishioners at the same church and following the harvest, I attended the same school in Cherry Tree Township.

That same spring I also met Willie Rynd. Rynd had just got done mixing it up with a boy about twice his size. When the fisticuffs ended, Willie proved to be the victor and his bloody-nosed opponent hastily retreated into the woods beyond the Rynd farm. I had been fishing down at the creek when I witnessed the spectacle. Willie approached me shortly thereafter and commenced to challenge me to a duel of fists. I was shaking in my moccasins when he suggested that I was a companion of the big bully he had just roughed up. I did my best to convince him otherwise and after several minutes of pleading my case, he dropped his bloodied fists and introduced himself. I would later learn that Willie was much like Johnny Steele. He was a courageous fellow and his only fear appeared to be attending school. Willie's primary passion was fighting and getting lost in the woods while book 'larning' made him shrivel and cringe. Willie once confessed that reading and writing for him was the equivalent of pouring salt on a slug. Like Steele, he was lanky and athletic and possessed impressive strength for a boy of 13 years. And though he cared little for schooling, he was quick- witted and usually possessed good common sense. Unlike Steele, who was very handsome, Willie looked like a horse. He had big, square front teeth and his upper lip curled back so far, that it touched the base of his nose. He had a head full of spindly, red hair and his pale face was covered with big, brown freckles. Though his appearance was not intimidating to say the least, the confidence he projected in both his physical dexterity and cool demeanor certainly was enough to stand down the nastiest of bullies. Willie lived on the farm about a mile above our place, near the mouth of Cherry Tree Run where it gushed into Oil Creek. It was even larger than the McClintock Farm and since Willie's only sibling was a younger sister, a couple of hired hands helped him and his Father work the farm.

Then there was Tommy Blood. The Blood Farm was located several hundred yards east of Rynd Farm. Tommy was nearly identical to me in both stature and demeanor. We were both pudgy and flat-footed, but what we lacked in physical agility and stamina, we made up for in intelligence. And though we weren't daring and reckless, we both enjoyed school and learning and believed in challenging our brains. There was never any tension between Tommy and me as there was between Steele and Rynd. Though Johnny and Willie were not mortal enemies, there was a confliction in their personas that caused friction between them. And they subconsciously or consciously avoided one another at all costs.

And though Tommy and I eventually considered ourselves intellectuals amongst a hamlet of barbarians, we still appreciated the grandeur of the Allegheny foothills and the great fishing that was prevalent in the area. Of course, there wasn't much else for a boy to do when not attending school or doing chores. Tommy would later introduce me to many of the other local children including Benji Tarr and Jimmy Miller. There were also plenty of girls in the valley, but I didn't pay them any mind until later.

CHAPTER 3

One summer morning while gigging for fish near Glen Barker's place, I was drawn to something on the hillside above. It was the crackling of a fire and thick plumes of gray smoke were filtering through the trees. I tossed aside my spear and shinnied up the steep embankment some fifty yards until I reached a smoldering fire-pit and a large, hastily constructed lean-to. I nosed around the site for a few minutes until I reckoned that it had been abandoned. The only thing that appeared to have been left behind was a rusty, old pale that contained a quart of fermenting blackberries.

As I tossed some dirt onto the fire to choke out the last remnants of flames, I was startled by something in the woods beyond the campsite. The shadowed figure of a man was approaching through the thick, green vegetation. I grew a bit nervy when I suspected it might be ornery old Glen Barker himself, but a moment later a strikingly handsome gent of about 20 stepped out into the clearing. I believe he was more startled then me, for in one hand he held a collection of poetry and with the other, he was fumbling to button his britches. Once he accomplished securing his pants, he tossed the book aside and stretched his arms above his head and sighed in relief.

We eyeballed one another rather awkwardly before he smiled and greeted me. "Howdi! I just got done relieving myself in the world's biggest outhouse," he snickered before turning and plopping down onto the ground in front of his poorly constructed shelter. I just stood there and gawked, still a bit startled by his presence. " Wasn't expectin' company. Had I known, I would have caught us a rabbit or something, because the fish certainly aren't biting. Anyway, name's Sam," he proclaimed as he reached for the pale of berries. "And you are?" I finally broke the ice, "I'm Andrew Buchanan. I live up the creek a ways." I then pointed to the north. He smiled and reached into the pale recovering a handful of the gooey berries. "Got some berries here. Want some?" he asked before cramming them into his mouth. I politely refused, and watched as he quickly devoured four or five more handfuls. I saw the disappointment in his purple and red stained face when he emptied the pale. He mentioned that he had done some fishing on the previous evening, but had no luck. "The creek is to low. You gotta spear'em or use a net to catch them," I informed him.

I then told Sam that though most of the farmers in the valley wouldn't be bothered by his harmless intrusion, old man Barker didn't take kindly to trespassers, and that he would most likely be greeted with a heavy dose of rock salt from Barker's musket if he got caught. I assisted Sam in tearing down the shelter and burying the smoldering coals of the fire. Figuring that he had no place to go for the time being, and that he probably hadn't had a good meal in quite some time, I offered him dinner at the Buchanan Farm. He initially refused my invitation. But I insisted. "Are you sure that your family won't mind?" he asked while collecting the few belongings that were strewn about the thick underbrush. "Nah. They like company," I reassured him as he rolled his meager possessions up in a blanket and tied them off with a piece of twine. We then stumbled and slid our way down the steep incline before reaching the creek bank.

In the short amount of time it took us to get to the farm, I had already grown quite fond of Sam. He possessed a free spirit and had a wonderful, if not unusual, sense of humor. He spoke so gracefully that the words just seemed to flow from his mouth. I could sense that he possessed a superior intelligence. Yet with all that, there was still a great amount of humility about him.

Later that afternoon, after we dined on smoked ham, roasted potatoes, and freshly baked bread, I introduced Sam to nearly everyone in the valley. And just like me, everyone took an instant liking to this carefree spirit. The Rynd family even asked him to be there guest until he was to catch his steamship a few days later.

It turned out that at 19 years of age, Sam had already lived an exciting and adventurous life. He was also very good at recollecting such. Mr. Rynd was skeptical of some of Sam's claims, but admitted that the lad was a wonderful storyteller. On the evening prior to Sam's departure, Jonathon Rynd sponsored a pig roast that everyone in the valley was invited too. Nearly a hundred people showed up for the feast and it wasn't long before Buchanans, McClintocks, Millers, Tarrs, Bloods and Rynds gathered around the giant bonfire to listen to Sam's stories.

He told amazing tales of growing up along a mighty river, one that was several times larger than our own Allegheny. On this great river he caught catfish as big as hogs and had encounters with pirates and bandits that pillaged and looted local villages. He spoke of deep, dark caves nestled in the river bluffs where the pirates used to stash their gold. He also told us about piloting a riverboat to a city so far south, that giant Alligators patrolled the murky, warm waters and often devoured the unsuspecting bather. His stories were nearly as fascinating as the young man himself and upon his departure the following day, a subtle despair settled over our little community. Strangers were not uncommon as the occasional carpetbagger or hobo would straggle into the area, but this particular stranger had brought some excitement to our uneventful, monotonous lives.

CHAPTER 4

A week or so after Sam's departure, I grew a bit discouraged because the dry, hot spell continued. It had been nearly two weeks since the last rain and the creeks were so low that they were merely trickling down their stony paths. The fishing was terrible and the farmers, including my Father, were extremely concerned because the harvest was less than a month away. Old Jimmy Buchanan's temper was rising as fast as the mid day thermometer, therefore after completing my chores, I put a good deal of distance between us until suppertime.

Fortunately for me, our neighbors had convinced my Mother that marauding Indians and bloodthirsty panthers no longer prowled the surrounding hills and I was no longer confined to the outskirts of our property or the banks of Oil Creek. I later recalled one of the local boys speaking of a small, spring fed pond that was hidden on the hillside between the

Rouse and Barker farms. He claimed that it was full of yellow-bellied catfish and plump bream. I was suffering from a bad case of boredom, so I figured I'd give it a try. I grabbed my pole and another can of worms before making the quarter mile journey south along the ditch that used to be Oil Creek. Once I passed below Henry Rouse's property, I climbed over the dry, rocky embankment and pushed my way into the thick, steamy vegetation. Biting gnats and black flies brought as much discomfort as the 90 degree temperature.

I continued on through the thick growth of underbrush and mountain laurel until I finally reached an open plateau a few hundred yards above the creek. Dozens of thorn- apple trees and hundreds of berry bushes jetted out from the surrounding landscape. In the distance I could hear the sound of falling water and a melodic chorus of peep frogs. As I made my way through the thorny entanglement of the orchard I was suddenly startled by a large covey of grouse bursting through the brush. I watched as the big birds took to the wing and quickly soared out of sight. When I continued on towards the sound of the cascading water, I caught a quick glimpse of a deer crossing through the meadow some distance ahead. The animal spotted me and bolted into the tree line on the opposite side. I felt in some strange way privileged because though whitetail deer used to be abundant in the area, a century of hunting for both sport and sustenance had nearly wiped them out.

When the deer bounded out of sight, I continued towards the meadow and paused to dine on the plump, succulent blackberries and raspberries that were everywhere. Even in the torrid heat, Nature had been generous enough to provide an abundance of sweet things. After getting my fill I proceeded through a half-acre plot of buttercup and wild daisy before I finally reached the small run of water that was gushing down over a steep, twenty-foot embankment. I figured that this was the runoff from the pond I had been looking for. Thoroughly parched, I dropped my fishing pole and cupped my hands into the cool, falling water. Within moments my bladder was full, so I recovered my pole and trudged up and over the rocky, 45 degree incline.

I was delighted as to what came next. The pond was larger than I had imagined, about 50 yards in diameter. The far (eastern) end was covered in cattail and skunk cabbage but the adjoining banks were virtually brush free. Several sprawling sugar maples on the opposite hillside provided shade and a cool, refreshing breeze pushed off the waters rippling surface. It appeared as though our mini-drought, which was drying out every other waterhole in the area, was having little effect on this particular oasis. Newts, tadpoles and other kinds of amphibians could be seen darting across the silt bottom and a small school of bream were patrolling the shallows. Moments later, the peepers started up again.

I quickly baited my hook and was about to toss in my line, when a movement on the far bank got my attention. A man was resting up against the massive trunk of an ancient maple tree. He had a black, stovepipe hat resting over his face. A fishing rod lay on the ground at his feet and a stringer of bullhead catfish was hanging from the limb above his head. The faint sound of his snoring could be heard amongst the noisy frogs.

From his physique, I knew it wasn't Glen Barker, and was for certain that it wasn't the industrious Henry Rouse. Rouse had no time for leisurely things, especially fishing. Just then a small pocket of gnats flew into my mouth, bounced off of my tonsils and caused me to choke. The hoarseness of my bellow quickly awoke the gentleman. I watched as he straightened his hat and then reached around to the opposite side of the tree and recovered a short barreled musket. I nearly messed my pants when he jumped up in a defensive posture and peered around the surrounding countryside. I began shaking in my shoes when I sensed that I was about to be shot. Just when I was about to drop my pole and run, he spotted me. He wiped the sleep from his beady eyes and placed the gun back up against the tree.

"Hey boy! Didn't know I was havin' company!" he hollered. " Come on over!" I was reluctant at first. In the six months that we had lived in the valley I had met nearly everyone that called it home. However I didn't recognize this fellow. He was meager in stature and of average height. His scraggly, graying beard and weathered face revealed that he was at least 60 years of age. "Come on boy! Don't be afraid. This holes big enough for the both of us!" he insisted. Against my better judgment I slowly made my way around the pond. I figured that if he were going to shoot me, he would have already done so. After the greetings, he pointed out the spot were he had already landed six nice catfish. I cast in my line, but when my worms were failing to get a fish to bite, the old man handed me a piece of bait that resemble a cube of aging cheese. The stuff reeked of something awful. I carefully baited my hook with it and tossed in my line. Not two minutes later a fish grabbed the bait and straightened my line. I set the hook and slowly reeled in the fish. To my surprise, a plump two pound, yellow-bellied catfish was plopping around at my feet. The old man shared in my excitement.

I spent the next hour fishing with Walter Tucker. He told me to call him 'Tuck'.

Tucker lived in a hollow roughly a mile or so through the woods. His little shanty sat along a torrent little stream known as 'Moody Run'. Moody Run drained into Cherry Run about a mile or so above the Buchanan Farm. In a short hour I learned that 'Tuck' was a trapper and relied solely on the land for his survival. He claimed that he had moved into the area only a year or two earlier, after spending much of his time out west. He spoke of hunting and trapping in the Rocky Mountains and working for the pony express. He even mentioned working alongside the likes of Kit Carson and Jedidiah Smith. When I asked him about the huge bear claw that hung from a beaded necklace around his neck, he said that it had belonged to the first 'grizzled bar' that he'd ever 'kilt'. He claimed that he killed the old bear with his bare hands, and a big knife. He then proceeded to show me a repaired (sown) tear in his linsey-woolsey shirt that he claimed was made by the bear.

Shortly before calling it a day, we heard a ruckus in the forest above the pond. Old Tuck reached for his musket again. We listened as tree limbs were being flung back and forth and a muffled noise, similar to the drumming of a grouse, echoed through the hillside. A few minutes later it stopped and the birds returned to chirping and singing. But Tucker kept his old musket at the ready. I sensed some serious paranoia about this aging soul. When I suggested that it was probably just a couple of gray squirrels playing in the trees or the deer that I had spooked earlier, he wouldn't have any of it. "Nope!" He adamantly proclaimed while scanning the surrounding terrain. "Smell that?" he quietly asked. "Smell what?" I remarked. "Take a whiff." he demanded. I then took a deep breath and realized what he was talking about. It was a pungent, musky odor, like that of a skunk. Then the wind shifted and the smell subsided.

Tuck eventually relaxed and then told me about an old Indian legend. He claimed that a 'wild man' roamed these hills. He also believed that he was being stalked by this so-called 'wild man'. His story was beginning to scare me and to alleviate my fear I suggested that what we had smelled was the decomposing plant matter and skunk cabbage that was prevalent amongst the cattails on the far bank. Tuck just snickered, gathered up his musket and fishing rod and claimed that he was going home to have a drink of whiskey.

Over the course of the next week, I met Tuck everyday at my new favorite fishing hole. I was often rewarded with a creel of tasty catfish and bream and the old man's entertaining stories. One afternoon I followed him to his little homestead in Moody Run Hollow. He had actually constructed two small shanties from the weathered planks of an old, dilapidated barn that he found in Plummerville. The larger of the two was his living quarters and contained a cot, some dusty blankets and a shelf that contained several candles and a couple jars of whiskey. The other shanty had several iron traps hanging from the walls and some strange contraptions that Tuck claimed was used for stretching skins. In the far corner of the darkened building was another large contraption that had coiled, copper tubing dangling from the top of it. Dozens of mason jars and gallon jugs lined the shelves along the walls. I also spotted two large baskets of freshly picked apples on the floor in the opposite corner. "Help yourself!" Tuck said, "I won't be needin' all of them." In no time I devoured three of the crunchy fruit.

I followed Tuck up onto the ridge above his homestead where we were standing amongst dozens of large, moss-covered boulders. He led me to a spot where three of the big, gray stones rested against one another. Tuck claimed that it was his secret vault and that I was the only one in the whole world, other than him, that knew about it.

He declared that I was a good friend and could be trusted. "I want to show you something," he said as he reached his hand deep into the stony enclave. I cringed with the thought of a rattlesnake hiding from within, but without incident he retrieved what he was looking for. He then reached into a large, wool sock that was saturated with a greasy substance and removed a shiny, multi-barreled pistol. Tuck buffed it with his shirt and handed it to me. I was awestruck by the beautiful piece. It was a .32 caliber pepperbox pistol with an engraved, gold-plated frame. The gun was old but looked as though it had never been fired. There wasn't a scratch on it. Tuck kept it coated with whale oil and wrapped in the sock to keep it from rusting. He didn't carry it because he was afraid it would get lost or rust away to nothing. "Besides," he claimed, "my musket does everything I ask it to."

He received the treasured, heirloom from his Father, while he was on his deathbed. "Yep! I'll never part with it. Not until my dieing day!" he claimed before admiring it some more. Shortly thereafter he returned it to the sock and stuffed it back in the rocky vault. I thanked him for the hospitality and returned home for supper.

CHAPTER 5

The rain came and the temperatures dropped back down to the seasonal norm. One late summer morning, Wille Rynd suggested we do some exploring. He wanted to investigate a tiny island on Oil Creek about a half of mile below the Buchanan Farm. I was a little reluctant at first because Johnny had pointed it out to me earlier in the summer and claimed that it was infested with snakes. Willie said that was nonsense and reassured me that we would be safe, and home in time for supper.

We started at the mouth of Cherry Run and trudged our way along the banks of the creek careful not to step on a rattlesnake. Fortunately for us the dry spell had ended and the venomous critters were retreating back into the thick cover of the wooded hills, where they holed up in rocky crevices and abandoned burrows. On occasion I would see a silly looking fish feeding in the shallows. The foot long sucker had a rectangular shaped head and was blotted with square patches of green and brown. Once spooked, the lightning fast fish would disappear into the deeper, turbulent water. Willie called them 'stony pokers'. He claimed they were bottom feeders that dined on the plant life that grew on the creek bottom. I think he read my mind when he remarked, "They aint much for eatin' though". There was however plenty to eat along the broadening creek bank. Thick, fibrous branches of ripened elderberry reached out amongst the coiled, thorny vanes of blackberry and raspberry. Acres of blueberry and currant bushes flourished on the rocky outcroppings a little ways beyond the rising embankment. Willie permitted me a few moments to graze amongst the sweet fruit before his impatience demanded that we move on.

So we splashed onward and upon clearing a bend in the waterway, our destination came into view. The creek widened to over a hundred yards and then branched off into two directions. One arm of the turbulent waters continued south while the other veered to the west. They conjoined a couple of hundred yards later and continued the three mile push to the Allegheny. Right in the middle of the churning waterway stood our island. The two acre plot of land was encompassed by a sandy, gravel beachhead. Thick strands of poverty grass and delicate moss covered the ground not littered in stones. The interior of the island was hidden from view by a thick, green fauna and several ancient sycamores that were spread out along the perimeter.

Blue herons and kingfishers strolled along the bank searching for lunch of small fish and crustaceans. The hoarse squawking of more herons could be heard from within the interior of the isolated landmass. We were careful to cross some waist deep rapids but it wasn't long before I took the first plunge. The slick rocks on the creek bed made for difficult footing and I struggled to recover my feet. Willie laughed at my clumsiness and then plunged into the water himself. A minute later he came up for air and held a huge crayfish in his hand. He subsequently tossed the brawny clawed creature in my direction and I scampered to avoid being hit. I watched as the big, beady- eyed crustacean darted backwards through the water before disappearing into a rocky crevice.

I continued my struggle across the turbulent water and upon our arrival at the island, was much fatigued. I threw myself down upon the coarse ground and remained there until I caught my wind. Willie, less exhausted, plopped down beside me. While staring up into the clear, late morning sky, I asked him if the place had a name. " No! Not that I'm aware of anyway. It's just an overgrown sandbar," he said as he stood to his feet. " Come on! I got something to show you," he proclaimed before he slapped the sand and dirt from the back of his britches. "What about Heron Island?" I asked as I got up and brushed off my own pants. "Gosh Drew. Could you be anymore creative?" he sarcastically remarked. "Call it whatever you want," he added before making our way across the beach. As we pushed through the thick fauna and into the coolness of the shade trees we were greeted with the raspy chatter of cicadas and crickets. Continuing on, I carefully watched my step because I remembered what Johnny had told me about the snakes.

Once we stepped through the column of sycamores the ground was thick with ferns and sticky shrubs. It wasn't long before we were standing in the center of the semi-darkened island. I felt very insignificant and minute when I peered up and realized we were standing amongst a jury of giants. The coolness that the canopy of the massive trees provided brought some relief to my hot, sunburned face. I watched as Willie began shoving aside some ferns along the base of one of the trees. " I know you're in here somewhere," he said to himself as hopped from tree to tree, kicking aside the shrubs and brush. "Aha! I found you!" he proclaimed moments later, bringing an end to his desperate search. I could see the excitement in his chaffed face.

I ambled over to where Willie stood and was amazed as too what I saw next. Leaning up against the trunk of the tree was a giant piece of slate-like rock. The mass was longer than I was tall and roughly three foot in height. But what was so fascinating about the huge fragment was what it contained. The darkened impression etched in the stone resembled the skeleton of some large serpent. Its large, pointed skull was as long as my forearm and the mouth was full of sharp, dagger-like teeth. The neck was even longer and it was swept back against the wolf-sized body. The torso was flanked by four stubby legs and long talons were attached to the toes. The tail was longer than the neck and body combined and was swept back against the underside of the thing.

"What is it?" I asked as we loomed over the mass. "My Pa called it a 'fossil.' He said that this animal lived a long, long time ago. He called it Nature's artwork." Willie said as he kneeled down and brushed away some of the dry moss that was covering the surface. "It does kind of look like a painting," I declared as I tried to visualize what this critter looked like when it was alive. A sudden chill came over my body and I shivered as I peered around the surrounding terrain. "What are you doing?" Willie asked while noticing the somewhat frightful concern on my face. " Could them things still live here?" I asked as the goose bumps began to muster on my portly arms.. "No. This thing was probably buried for a hundred years." Willie then explained to me that he found the fossil during the previous summer. His Father, who was an intelligent man and historian, told him that the relic was probably dredged up along the creek during a recent ice jam, which was common along Oil Creek during the late winter season. The force exerted from the flow of these massive sheets of ice uprooted the rock and carried it downstream before depositing it against the base of the tree.

"We thought about taking it home, but that thing weighs a ton," Willie noted. Upon closer examination, he was probably right. The piece of stone canvass that

Nature had used to create her masterpiece was about seven inches thick. I figured it would take three or four strong men and a team of oxen to load and transport it. I was still a bit uneasy about hanging out on the island and eventually convinced Willie that it was time to go.

CHAPTER 6

As we left the island and started back across the churning water, I spotted something in the distance. Along the opposite bank about a hundred yards below, was a tiny, black in color object bobbing with the current. It appeared to be caught up in a snag created by the roots of a fallen tree. I pointed it out to Willie who just shrugged it off as nothing. I told him that I was going in for a closer look and then stumbled and sloshed my way down the creek. When I finally reached the snag I spooked a couple of cows that were along the edge of the water. An old heifer bellowed before they turned and moseyed back onto a nearby farm.

A closer inspection revealed the object to be a torn and tattered stovepipe hat. I recognized it as belonging to Walter Tucker. Willie eventually made his way to the snag and climbed through the entangled roots to retrieve the old hat. He tossed it to me and claimed it would be good kindling material once it dried out. "This is Walter Tucker's hat," I declared as I squeezed the water from the worn, felt-like brim. "Do you mean that old, slimy squatter that lives along Moody Run?" Willie asked in disgust. I was a bit taken back by his comment. I had found a wonderful friend and fishing partner in Ole' Tuck. "He isn't slimy and he ain't no squatter!" I snapped as I continued wringing water from the hat. "I wonder why he left it?" I asked myself before placing it upon my head. Willie smirked, "He was probably down here fishing and had a few too many snootfuls. The old drunk probably didn't even realize he left it behind." I gave Willie a disgruntled sigh before we made our way back up the creek.

On the following morning I finished my chores early and retrieved the hat from our shed. I had left it hanging overnight, hoping that it would dry out. My plan worked, it was as dry as a desert. I then made the mile long trek through the wooded hills to Ole' Tuck's place. When I reached the small wooden shanties, there was no sign of Walter Tucker anywhere. I hollered his name a few times but got no response. I then pushed open the front door of his little house and cautiously stepped inside. In the semi-darkness I could see that his cot was bare. Two dusty blankets were strewn across the dirty, plank wood floor and the old woodstove looked like it hadn't been used for cooking in quite some time. Sunlight began filtering through a gaping hole in the ceiling where the flue had once been. The tin exhaust pipe was now a mangled piece of scrap lying against the far wall. I also noticed a few broken jars scattered about the floor and started to feel a bit nauseated from the faint odor of stale whiskey. I then determined that the place had been ransacked.

I stepped back outside and made my way to the other shanty that Tuck used for storage. I slowly pushed open the door and another burst of sunlight illuminated the musty room. The funny contraption with the coiled copper tubing was still nestled on the floor alongside a big, wooden apple press. Two large baskets of fermenting apples that were buzzing with honeybees and fruit flies sat behind the contraptions while piles of dried cornhusks cluttered the remaining floor space. Everything seemed in order, or at least as I could recall from my last visit. Upon exiting the little shanty an afterthought came to mind. I stepped back inside the shanty and peered around the dust-laden walls. Tuck's traps were gone.

At first I reasoned that the old trapper was out setting his line but then I recalled him mentioning that the season didn't start until after the first good freeze. He claimed that early November was a good time because the animals had their full winter coats.

Any earlier and the pelts weren't of any value. I was stumped because it was still early in September. I felt some relief when I noticed that his fishing rod and tackle were also missing. "Maybe he moved his traps and is just out doing some fishing," I mumbled to myself as I reached into one of the baskets of apples and dug around until I found a good one. I took a big bite from the juicy piece of fruit and made my way back outside. I then removed the hat from my head and hung it on the wooden peg where Tuck usually hung his skin stretcher.

Just as I was about to make my way down Moody Run and return home, an unusual sensation came over me. I couldn't figure out what it was but a sudden chill flared up my goose bumps. I dropped the apple core to the ground and was suddenly smitten with fear. My sixth sense kicked in when I felt as though I were being watched. Moments later a strong pungent odor, like that at the pond, whirled in the gentle breeze. I was eventually able to reassure myself that I was just being foolish and had nothing to worry about. But when I started back down the run, a terrifying, bone-chilling scream echoed through the hollow. It was god awful, unlike any wild animal I had ever heard. It was almost human, like that of a woman screaming in agony, only higher in pitch. When I turned to locate the origin of the frightening sound I observed a dark, hairy figure maneuvering through the mountain laurel about a hundred yards above me. My heart raced when I could hear the busting of brush and limbs and the distant sound of heavy footsteps. Fortunately for me, the man-sized apparition was retreating into the dense undergrowth of the forest. I turned and high-tailed it for Cherry Run. And though I was knocked-kneed and flatfooted, I made record time to the farm.

I tried to convince myself that I had merely seen a bear. After all, Johnny and I had a close encounter with a large bruin earlier in the spring, less than a mile away. Yet this thing didn't move like a bear, it was more human-like. And the scream that made my blood curdle certainly didn't belong to a black bear. My first thought was to tell my terrifying encounter to Johnny, therefore I dashed over to the McClintock Farm. Unfortunately Mrs. McClintock informed me that Johnny had gone along with his Stepfather to Meadeville to purchase some farming implements. She said that they'd be there for a couple of days. I then made my way to the Rynd Farm and was relieved to find Willie there. When I conveyed my story to him, he argued that I had seen a bear. When I strongly rejected his conclusion, he smirked and asked me what I thought I'd actually seen. I hesitated and was almost reluctant to say. When he asked again, I cleared my throat and announced, "The Wild Man." "What? Do you honestly believe in that old Indian tale?" he asked before shaking his head in total disbelief. I then told him about Tuck's claim that the Wild Man was stalking him and I was worried that the beast may have been the cause of the old trapper's sudden disappearance. "The only thing that old squatter disappeared into was a jar of corn mash whiskey," he remarked sarcastically.

The concern on my face finally got the best of my bucked-tooth friend. I also believe that my so-called foolish revelation may have ignited the adventurous flame that loomed from within his young, muscular frame. Willie's reckless spirit was also a prideful one and the idea of winning a confrontation with my so-called beast, would jettison him above Johnny Steele in regards to popularity, especially with the local girls.

On the day following my eerie encounter, Willie and I met up at Cherry Run. Willie had brought along his trusty longbow and a half-dozen, razor-sharp arrows that were crammed into a rawhide quiver. The powerful bow had been fashioned from a hickory stave by old Stephen Irwin. Irwin operated a lumber mill in Cherry Tree Township and was a master woodworker and bowyer. The arrows were crafted from cedar and the points were forged of iron. Some file work finished the deadly arrowheads. I thought about taking a gun. My father owned a shotgun, but I reckoned that my mother would have thrown a fit if she caught me trying to sneak it out of the house. Therefore my weapon of choice was the pitchfork I borrowed from Henry Rouse's barn.

As we left Rouse' property and ventured forward into the forest, I grew a bit nervy as to what might lie ahead. Flashbacks from the previous afternoon lingered in my mind and though I only caught a glimpse of whatever I saw, my wild imagination was doing a good job filling in the rest. A recollection of the old trapper's story had convinced me that something awful was looming in the local hills. And that his disappearance was directly linked to whatever was roaming the woods near Moody Run

Hollow. Willie noticed the nervous, apprehension in my gait and reassured me that we had nothing to fear. "It's probably just a darned groundhog anyway," he sarcastically stated as we trudged forward. We followed Cherry Run to Moody Run and then made the half-mile trek up the narrow hollow. When we arrived at Tuck's place nothing had changed from the previous day. His shanty home was still a mess and the cookstove was cold to the touch. We nosed around for several minutes before Willie declared that the old squatter had probably wandered off into the woods to die. Upset by Rynd's insensitive remark, I ventured over to Tuck's shed and retrieved the hat that I had hung there the previous day. I tossed the pitchfork on the ground at my feet and placed the hat upon my head. I then climbed up the steep, rocky slope, and plopped down on a small boulder to sulk. Willie recognized my sullen state and awkwardly approached me. With some remorse in his voice he told me that men like Walter Tucker never stay put for very long. He believed that Tuck had packed his most important possessions and moved on.

I appreciated Willie's honest conclusion and nearly accepted it as reasonable explanation when one final thought came to my head. I scanned the surrounding hillside until I spotted what I was looking for. "Come on!" I shouted and dashed through the woods until I reached the rocky vault. Willie, curious about my excitement, followed. I tossed aside some brush and started to reach into the stony crevice before I abruptly retracted my arm. "Grab a stick," I ordered.

Willie reached into the quiver that was slung on his back and removed an arrow. I grabbed the arrow and immediately thrust it into the crevice where I poked around for a few seconds. Satisfied that a snake was not hiding within, I reached back into the rocks and to my surprise, recovered Tuck's pepperbox pistol, it was still wrapped in the sock. Willie was fascinated with the shiny, multi-barreled handgun. "Wow, I could use this for blasting critters," he boasted while cocking the hammer and snapping the trigger. I snatched the pistol back from him. This find convinced me that Tuck had not left on his own free will. There was no way the old trapper would have knowingly left behind this valuable heirloom. Willie eventually agreed. "Listen, I know some people who might know where Tucker went. Let's get home too supper, and tomorrow, after doing our chores, we can call on some of them," Willie declared before I wrapped the gun up in the sock and crammed it back into the stony vault. "But, if I help you and we never find the old squatter, the fancy pistol is mine. Do you agree?" I was a bit angered by his gesture. "You were going to help me anyway'," I reminded him. "Do you agree?" he repeated. I reluctantly nodded in agreement. "But don't shortcut me on this one. I want to find my friend," I snapped at him. "Deal!" Willie replied.

CHAPTER 7

I arose to a heavy downpour. Just after sunup my chores were complete and the rain had subsided. I journeyed down to the mouth of Cherry Run to wait on Willie. It was quite chilly and a light fog covered the valley corridor. I crotched down on the ground and was entertained by a family of raccoons skirting along the opposite bank. Momma was in the lead with her four babies tailing right behind. Their bellies were full from an evening smorgasborg of crayfish and frogs. The fury little critters eventually disappeared from sight. Moments later I spotted the faint outline of a boy floating down Oil Creek on a raft. I could see the long pole in his hands that was used to steer free from snags and guide the vessel. Willie eventually broke through the fog and guided the wooden craft to my position along the bank. Though it was still very early, Willie was very much awake and ready to go. I climbed aboard and upon closer examination, was quite impressed with what I saw. "Dang, Willie.

This is some boat," I proclaimed as I took up a seat. "Yeah, me and Mister Irwin built it about a month ago. But the cricks been so dang low, I ain't had it out," he declared as we shoved off from the bank.

All of the rain from the previous two days had elevated the creek level about a foot and the water itself was the color of mud. Yet with all of the churning, mucky turbulence, it made for a pleasant ride. We cruised past Heron Island and steered clear of a fallen tree just below Ham McClintock's farm. We continued on another hundred yards when a house and barn on the plateau above the creek, came into view. Two large cornfields sat to the north and south of the whitewashed structures and several head of livestock grazed freely in the crop fields. About the time I was going to ask about the huge spread, Willie interrupted, "That's Shem Clives' place. Talk is that he's the one who supplies your friend with the corn and apples to make hard cider and whiskey." I had never met Clives and never heard his name mentioned, which was unusual in such a tight knit community. I conveyed that thought to Willie. A wide grin came about his freckled face. "That's because the womenfolk despise him, and your old squatter. The menfolk appreciate them though. Clives' ingredients and Tuckers' recipes keep the farmers happy on dreary days. Yep! Ole' Tuck's concoctions have created some harsh exchanges between the valley's husbands and wives," Willie declared. "The devil lurks in these hills, and he disguises himself in old, fruit jars. At least, that's what my mother says," he added with a snicker.

"Maybe Clives knows of Tuck's whereabouts! Can we get over in time?" I asked realizing that the current had picked up and jettisoned us into deeper, more turbulent water. Without a response, Willie struggled mightily to get control of the raft and direct it through the churning rapids. He struggled mightily with the guide pole but eventually freed us from the current and steered us ashore. Upon tying the raft to an overhanging tree limb, we shinnied up the steep, earthy embankment and stepped onto a trail that ran the length of the creek. An approaching wagon could be heard in the distance. As we walked along the trail to get to Clives' farm, the wagon pulled up alongside. A scraggly looking fellow halted his team of horses. I recognized him as Glen Barker. Barker spit a wad of tobacco juice at our feet and then wiped his nappy, graying beard with his scrawny forearm. "Whud yins boys doin' down hur?" he asked with a detested look about his pock-marked face. As I recoiled in either fear or disgust, Willie stepped forward. "We are looking for Walter Tucker. Have you seen him about, Mister Barker?" the boy asked without a hint of intimidation. Barker spit again before contemplating his next response.

" Nope. I ain't nocare, no how. If 'ins the old bootlegger be gone, than good riddance! He be needin' to make a good livin' no how!" the illiterate old codger declared before grabbing the reins and directing his team back up the trail.

" He isn't to kindly, is he?" I noted as we watched the wagon disappear around a bend. "Nope! My Ma called him a 'recluse', whatever that is. She claims Mister Clives is one too, but he ain't as ornery," Willie replied before we turned and continued on. It wasn't long before we were climbing another steep hillside that rose about a hundred feet above the creek. We walked across a long, wooded plateau and onto Clives' property. I was nervous about entering onto his land but Willie assured we'd be fine. He claimed that Shem and his Father had done some horse-trading in the past. We followed a narrow path through a big cornfield before reaching Clives' house. It was a large, two story home that had the luxury of a raised front porch. We climbed several, creaky steps before reaching the front door. A mangy, hound was asleep in the far corner of the porch. The snoring canine didn't even acknowledge our presence. Without hesitation, Willie knocked. A few more raps and we heard the heavy footsteps from someone inside, approaching the door. "Who is it?" a deep voice bellowed. " It's Willie Rynd!" the boy hollered back. The door slowly pushed open.

Standing in the doorway was a big, stocky fellow of about 40 years. He had a wiry mustache and a thick, bushy brow. He immediately recognized Willie and greeted him with a big, toothless smile. " Willie Rynd" he declared, "how's your family?" Willie grinned and told him that they were fine. "Is your Pa still raising thoroughbreds?" Willie nodded his head in agreement and his grinned widened, "He's going to give me my very own Palomino, next year, for my birthday!" "Ain't that something!" Clives jubilantly shouted. The big fellow then peered at me. " I didn't know you had a brother?"

Somewhat intimidated by the massive man, I could say nothing. " No. This is Andrew Buchanan. His family just moved here in March. They live up the crick, near Henry Rouses' place." Clives acknowledged me with another toothless smile before questioning the purpose of our visit. "We was wondering if you've seen Walter Tucker thereabouts?"

Willie asked. A surprised look came upon Clives round, mottled face. He stared down at the warped, floorboards and thought for a moment. " Nope. Can't say as I have. Ain't see him in awhile." Clives then adjusted his britches and tightened the soiled, wool shirt around his thick torso. He then suggested that Walt was out looking for a wife and declared that he, himself, should be out courtin' one also. Shem claimed that life around the farm was growing quite lonely and that he'd trade most of his pigs for a good wife.

Somewhat discouraged, I turned and made my way down from the porch. Willie thanked Clives for his hospitality and followed. " But hey! When you do find him, let him know I got that bushel of apples he's been wanting. That old cuss must bake a lot of pies!" Clives hollered before returning inside the house. "He bakes pies alright!" Willie sarcastically remarked before we made our way back to the creek.

CHAPTER 8

"I don't understand it. Someone has to know where Tuck is. I mean he wouldn't just pick-up and leave without telling me. And he wouldn't have left his beloved pistol behind." I said as we climbed back aboard the raft. Willie then fell into deep thought. A moment later he returned. "Did he ever mention an Indian buddy to you?" Willie asked me. " No. Not that I recall. I mean, he told a few stories about fighting injuns when he was a young fellow. Why?" I asked. "There's an Indian that lives down at the village. I think his name is 'Graceful Bird'or something. Anyway, rumor has it that he helps Tucker with his trap line and making whiskey." I was somehow uplifted by the boys' revelation. The village of which Willie was speaking of was located at the confluence of Oil Creek and the Allegheny River. I had only been there once, earlier in the summer, when I rode along with my Father to purchase some provisions. We didn't stay long, so I didn't get to look around much. A decade later, this sprawling village would become the center of the new oil trade. They'd call it 'Oil City'.

Willie pushed us back out into the current and rode the rapids another mile or so until we neared the mouth of Oil Creek. About a hundred yards above the Allegheny we got stuck on a rocky snag. While Willie worked hard to free us, I was awestruck as to what I saw. To the northwest stood a rocky bluff, several stories high. Occasionally a boulder would plummet down the wide cliff-face and crash onto the ground above us. "Why hadn't I noticed this before, when I came along with my Pa?" I quietly asked myself. Of course my vantage point was different this time. The only thing more impressive than being directly below a giant bluff is standing atop of one. Willie was becoming frustrated with his seemingly fruitless effort in freeing us. The bottom rungs of the raft had gotten wedged between two submerged boulders and the pressure from the churning water was beginning to snap the sturdy boards. Willie told me to quit staring into space and shoved me off the raft. I reluctantly plunged in the waist deep water and struggled to reach the bank some 20 yards away. Willie tried one last time to hoist the raft from the snag, and when he did, the current grabbed hold. The little flat boat flipped over end and was thrust downstream by the rushing water. We could only watch, as moments later the splintered and tattered remains drifted into the depths of the murky, Allegheny.

When a frustrated and exhausted Willie finally reached shore, he plopped down beside me. I could see the anger in his sweaty, flushed face. "I hope for your sake we find that old squatter, because it took me and Mister Irwin a whole Saturday to build that boat!" Without saying a word, I continued to focus onto the huge bluff above us.

Eventually Willie's breathing settled and I figured that it was a good time to change the subject. "What's up there?" I asked pointing to the top of the cliff face. "Hogback," Willie replied as he got up and wrung the water from his linen shirt. "What?" I asked confused by his response. "You'll see what I'm talking about when we get to the village," he said before putting his shirt back on and climbing over the embankment. I got up, slapped the remaining water from my pant legs and followed.

The village consisted of several small homes and a few meager farms. A mercantile, grain and seed store and blacksmith shop sat right in the center of town. A whitewashed church with a crooked, weathered steeple stood on the hillside above the quiet village. I followed Willie down the main road into town until we reached another whitewashed building. From inside we could hear the loud clanging of iron against iron and watched as strands of slithering heat from the forge escaped through the seams in the walls. We stepped inside to find a middle-aged man of German descent hammering a piece of orange-hot iron on an anvil. We watched as he tossed aside the hammer and utilizing a pair of tongs, quenched the piece of molten metal in a vat of water. "What brings you boys here?" he asked without taking his eyes off of his work. "Well, Sir... before Willie could say another word, the Blacksmith stopped what he was doing and interrupted. "Willie Rynd?" he asked as he reached for his spectacles and fumbled to get them on his black, soot-covered face. "Does your Pa know you're here?"

"Nope, Mister Ausenfort, he doesn't," Willie replied, "But this is really important," he added. "Okay. What is it?" The man asked while using his grimy forearm to wipe the sweat from his bushy brow. Willie peered over at me and then to the Blacksmith. "My friend Andrew here, is worried about old Walter Tucker. Have you seen him?" Ausenfort thought it over for a moment while scratching his sweaty armpits. "I haven't seen that old codger in months. But I reckon he'll be in soon because the fur season is not far off and his traps will probably need some mending." he said before recovering the hammer and getting back to work. " Mister Ausenfort, do you know where we can find Tuck's Indian friend, Graceful Bird?" Willie asked just before the hammer flattened out another piece of molten iron. The Blacksmith looked up and grinned. "Do you mean the fat Indian that stays at the Widow Walsh's place?" he asked with sarcastic grin on his face. "Sitting Duck is what the locals call him. There ain't nothing graceful about that bird, especially after he swills two or three jars of the rot-gut whiskey they make." The Blacksmith then asked Willie if Walter Tucker was the real reason he ventured so far from home. Willie answered in the affirmative, but the sarcastic grin remained on Ausenforts' face. "Well boys, I got three more horses to shoe today. I need to be gettin' back to work," he declared before hammering away.

As we left the blacksmith shop, Willie told me that Widow Walsh lived on a small farm near the church. Suddenly Willie's attention was averted to a pedestrian that was strolling along the opposite side of the main road. "Hi Willie!" hollered a pig-tailed girl of about thirteen. She quickly made her away across the muddy roadway and approached us with a big, toothy grin. Willie's face turned bright red and he then returned the smile. "How are you Mattie?" The toothy greetings continued on for several minutes before Willie finally introduced me. Her name was Matilyn Ausenfort, daughter of the Blacksmith, and now I understood the man's suspicion in regards to Willie's arrival in town. Rynd was two years my senior, and though I didn't pay no mind to girls yet, he did.

Mattie, as he addressed her, looked a lot like Willie. She could have probably passed for his sister. Bucked-tooth and freckled face, her auburn hair glistened beneath the pink bonnet she wore above her curls. I must admit though, there was something pleasing about her. She was spunky but sweet and I could see in her eyes that she adored my friend. Matilyn was also well endowed for a girl her age and I believe that the shapely figure she possessed was of great concern for her Father. The flirtations went on for a few more minutes before I reminded Willie that it was starting to get late and that we still had a long trek ahead. My impatience paid off, Matilyn requested that Willie accompany her to the annual Harvest Dance and upon another toothy exchange, bid us farewell.

We continued on through the village until we reached a ferry on the banks of the Allegheny. Willie tossed the pilot a dime before we boarded and were ferried across the swollen river on his dilapidated flat boat. Upon reaching the opposite bank, we journeyed another half of mile up a grassy slope until we reached the church with the crooked steeple. Beyond the church, at the crest of Seneca Hill, was the Widow Walsh's house. Hers' was an elegant, three story brick home surrounded by acres of delicately cropped grass and shrubbery. A large barn sat some fifty yards to the south.

We made our way to the front door and before he knocked, Willie warned me that the Widow was an elderly lady and terribly hard of hearing. After several hard raps on the door, a pleasant grayed-haired woman of seventy answered the door. Her dark, gray eyes lit up when she recognized Willie before embracing him in her frail, trembling arms.

Eleanor Walsh had been a teacher and had taught at the Cherry Tree Academy for 10 years before retiring in 1851. Before Willie became a habitual truant, he was one of her most cherished students.

I just couldn't believe the attention freckled face, bucked-tooth Willie was starting to get from women, both young and old alike. The Widow invited us in and served us up a warm plate of scrumptious chicken and dumplings. We were then treated to a piece of blackberry cobbler and a cool glass of milk to wash it down. While our food digested, Willie made small talk with our wonderful host and discovered that in deed an Indian was residing at the place, working as a farm hand. The Widow called him 'James'. We were shown to the back door where we stepped outside to a yard staggered with beautiful rose bushes and purple rhododendron. A rooster and some hens pecked at the ground near the brightly colored plants while a plump gobbler strutted nearby.

We made our way across the big back yard and into the huge, wooden structure of a barn. Several horses and some milk cows were confined in the stalls and were munching from troughs filled with grain and pillows of alfalfa and hay. At the far end of the long corridor beyond the stalls was the distinct sound of someone shoveling manure.

"Mister James!" Willie called out, his voice echoing off the walls. He shouted again and this time the place grew silent. We could hear the clang of the shovel hitting the ground. Moments later a round, robust man of about 50 approached us. In fluent english, he told us that the widow didn't like trespassers and demanded that we leave the barn. I cowered as the burly man started staggering up the corridor, but Willie stood his ground. Willie informed him that Mrs. Walsh had invited us in and directed us to the barn. "What do you want from me?" he asked impatiently.

CHAPTER 9

Young Willie Rynd had a hankering for nosing around someone's personal life without causing offense. The three of us took up a seat on some hay bales and engaged in conversation. Over the course of Willie's half hour interview, we discovered that James' Indian name was indeed 'Graceful Bird'. We were also wrong in our assumption that he had been a member of the Seneca or Iroquois Tribe that once thrived in the area. Graceful Bird's mother was Lakota, from the upper Missouri River region. His Father was a French-Canadian fur trapper who met his mother at a trading post in the mighty Sioux Nation of the Dakotas. Shortly after James was born, his mother contracted small pox and died. After spending the next several years living among the Lakota, his Father returned east in the hopes that James would be educated as a white man.

James' appearance certainly confirmed his story. His skin was olive rather than red and his eyes were green. His head was crowned with a greasy, tangled crop of black hair and there was no sign of facial hair. I almost laughed when I recalled the Blacksmith refer to him as Sittin' Duck, because that's exactly what he looked like. When he walked, he actually waddled, which was due in part to a bad case of the gout. He also had a big belly that bunched up into a ball when he sat down. His pockmarked-face was round and his long, pointed nose resembled a beak. He appeared to be even tempered, and this was a good thing for though he possessed some silly physical attributes, his broad shoulders were equipped with two powerful arms. James spoke for quite some time about his boyhood. He claimed that he inherited the name 'Graceful Bird' from his mother's people when he was very young. Apparently he had a beautiful singing voice and possessed great physical prowess for a boy.

Eventually Willie realized that it was getting late and got to the point of our visit.

When he questioned James about Walter Tuckers whereabouts, the half-breed claimed that he hadn't seen old Tuck in several months. He said they shared a trap line along the backwaters of Oil Creek during the previous winter and caught several nice beaver. James claimed that they sold the furs to a local trader, split the profits, and shared a jar of Tuck's corn-mash whiskey before going their separate ways.

James had even considered making the journey to Moody Run to see his old friend, but his painful condition (gout) was worsening. Willie then peered over at me and I could see the 'what's next' expression about his face. I finally broke my silence when Willie couldn't comprehend what I was thinking. I was a bit reluctant as to what came next because I didn't want to insult James' intelligence. With both James and Willie staring me down, I finally conjured up enough nerve to ask. "We need to know about the 'wild man'. You know, the one that ole' Tuck used to talk about."

James laughed and brown drool from chewing tobacco ran down the corners of his mouth. He wiped the juice with his sleeve, adjusted the wad of chaw in his jaw, and ceased with the laughter. "So, you want to know about Chiye-tanka?" he asked with a more serious expression about his sweaty face. "Shy, who?" a confused Willie asked. "Chiye-tanka (pronounced Shy-ah-tonka)," the half-breed repeated. James then went on to tell us that Chiye-tanka was a word used by the Lakota that meant 'Big, Elder Brother of the Forest.' He claimed that the term was as old as the people themselves and for many generations his people had reported encounters with a large, hairy man-like beast that roamed the woods surrounding their settlements. James also claimed that Chiye-tanka was more spirit than flesh and was only seen by his people on rare very occasions. Encountering one in the forest was considered an omen or a premonition of things to come.

When James questioned my curiosity about Chiye-tanka, I told him that I believed this creature had abducted Walter Tucker. James smirked and another river of juice rolled down across his chin. He then told us that though Chiye-tanka was intimidating in physical stature, he was a timid creature, and a caretaker of sorts, living in harmony with nature. I told him about Tuck's revelation and of my encounter at Moody Run. He gaffed off Tuck's claim, considering it nonsense created by a drunken, paranoid fool. But he seemed to take my encounter more seriously. "Chiye-tanka is usually harmless in the ways of men. But if he is offended, he can become angered and dangerous. Some of my mothers' people claimed that he is swifter than a deer and more powerful than the great white bear (grizzly) of the west." Goose bumps formed on my forearms as I imagined how frightening this thing could be. Willie, growing increasingly interested, jumped in on our conversation. "How does one go about offending this shy-thing?" he asked. James thought it over. "I suspect such things as the killing of forest animals out of greed instead of sustenance, or even offending Chiye-tanka himself. I know that Tucker had a pretty foul mouth when he got snookered up. He may have said something that angered the beast."

Though somewhat frightened by this revelation, I was starting to feel relatively comfortable in speaking with James and continued to prod him for information. "So you agree that Chiye-tanka may have taken Tuck? If so where can we find him?" I asked, a bit nervous about my assumption. James then suggested that since old Walter Tucker was a drifter, he probably just picked up and moved on. I then mentioned Tuck's pepperbox pistol, and how he wouldn't have left such a valuable family heirloom behind. A serious expression came over James' face and I could see that he was starting to take my suspicion seriously. "I guess anything is possible. Come, follow me." He said before leading us out of the barn and to the grassy slope in front of the Widow's house. From this vantage point we had a picturesque view of the surrounding terrain. "There, is where you can find Chiye-tanka," James said as he pointed to the northwest. A forested ridge sat atop the cliff face at the confluence of Oil Creek and the Allegheny. Right in the center of the mountain was a clearing, a large grassy knoll that extended several hundred feet up the ridge. A giant knob of boulders and scrub brush jetted out from the lush, green meadow. This huge finger of land was bordered by a gushing run of spring water to the west and extended as far as the eye could see to the north. "Hogback," Willie announced. I focused onto the terrain and could definitely see the resemblance to a swine's back. James recalled a story he'd heard a few years earlier. Two fishermen were down along the banks of the river and observed something unusual above them. They claimed that a 'man-bear' was standing high atop the bluff and started tossing wagon-sized boulders at them before they retreated into the safety of the village. He also claimed that there was an old legend about a young Seneca warrior who had an encounter with Chiye-tanka. James said that the Indian boy was hunting alone on Hogback when came upon what he thought was a bear feeding amongst some blueberry bushes. When he shot an arrow into the beasts' rump, the angry creature turned and ran down the frightened boy. It then carried the hunter to the edge of the mountain and was about to throw him into the river when something strange happened. Chiye-tanka displayed compassion by dropping the youngster onto the ground beside him. It yanked the arrow from its rear end and snapped it in two, like a twig, before ambling back into the forest. James also claimed that the young hunter was spiritually inspired by the encounter and later became a prominent religious man and prophet among his people. 'Handsome Lake' was also the half brother of a powerful Indian named John Abeel. Abeel was better known as Cornplanter, Chief of the Seneca people whom thrived in the region a century earlier.

While peering out over the panoramic view, I asked James what it would take to get this beast to release Tucker, if indeed he had him. He scratched his head and then his rump before contemplating an answer. He finally suggested that we make an offering. When Willie asked what kind of offering, James simply said, "something sweet." The half-breed claimed that Chiye-tanka was much like a bear in regards to his appetite. He said the beast was very fond of berries, tree sap, and the honey from beehives. James also noted that once in a while, when a melon or pumpkin turned of missing from the garden of a local villager, in good humor, the wild man of Hogback was usually to blame.

Prior to our departure from the Widow's farm, we thanked James for his hospitality. When he bowed his head in a gesture of good well, I noticed a necklace that poked out from under his heavy flannel shirt. A closer inspection revealed it to be a bear claw necklace, much like the one Tuck had worn. When James observed me examining it he quickly tucked it back under his shirt. A surprised expression came over his face as he quickly fastened the remaining buttons. We then finished our goodbyes and started down towards the river. Willie sensed the suspicion about my face when we reached the ferry. When he questioned the reason for such, I told him about the bear-claw necklace. "Drew, he's an Indian. That's the kinda stuff they wear. Would you rather see him shirtless, with a head full of feathers, or a deerskin loin cloth?" Willie smirked. "I don't know. It just don't make any sense." I replied as the big flat boat carried us across the water.

During the hour long journey home I devised a plan for Tuckers rescue. Willie was not overly excited about it and initially refused to participate. When I reminded him that the harvest was scant days away and that school was beginning soon, he started to listen to the voice of reason. I also reminded him about the shiny, pepperbox pistol and the notion that if we couldn't recover the old trapper, the pistol was his. Willie's eyes lit up and his spirit was rekindled.

Chapter 10

That evening, following supper, I received permission from my Mother to spend the next day and evening at the Rynd Farm. Willie was able to talk his parents into allowing to him to stay at our farm. Though I was concerned about our deceit, and the severe repercussions we would face if we got caught, in my mind, Walter Tucker's life depended on it. On the following morning I went out into the shed and gathered a jar of my Mother's blackberry preserves and a gallon jug of maple syrup. I carefully stuffed them into an old, tattered pillow case that already contained a tin cup, a spoon and a dozen corn-dodgers wrapped in paper. A rolled up blanket was draped over my back. Willie arrived at the farm carrying a saddlebag crammed full with ham sandwiches, a tinder kit and a candle lantern. A wool blanket was tied around his waist and his trusty bow with a quiver full of arrows was slung across his back. I questioned the necessity of the bow and reminded him of James' story about the young Seneca warrior. It didn't take much more convincing to get Willie to leave it behind. It was hidden in the shed.

We finally left the farm and crossed some shallow rapids of Oil Creek. Upon reaching the opposite side we shinnied up the earthy embankment and onto the trail that led down to the village. As usual, a heavy condensation and fog blanketed the valley. We followed the trail about two miles before reaching a large farm that sat on the plateau above us. The Clatt Farm was the jumping off point from civilization as we knew it. Beyond Mortimer Clatt's property stood thousands of acres of uninhabited land with steep wooded hills, deep dark draws, and treacherous ravines. Once we made our way across the farm, I plopped down on a decaying stump and caught my wind. Willie stopped momentarily and focused onto the surrounding terrain. He mentioned how eerie the woods appeared with the morning fog still enveloping the highlands. I peered into the forest ahead and had to agree with my friend. There was something unusually different about this stretch of woods. I could feel the goose bumps rising again.

With some reassurance from Willie, I was able to fight off my fear and venture forward. We pressed through some thick vegetation in the form of mountain laurel before reaching our first summit. We then crossed through a narrow draw before trudging up another steep hillside. An hour later we reached our first destination, Foster's Corner. From there we would change direction and head south another two miles until we reached Hogback. Once Willie made it clear that we were beginning our ascent up the mountain, I started to grow a bit nervy. I reminded myself that we were miles away from civilization and in uncharted territory.Worst of all, we were nearing the domain of Chiye-tanka.

Not only was fear hampering my progress, but the weight of the goods I was hauling was causing much strain on my pudgy legs. Willie alleviated some of the strain by carrying the gallon jug of syrup for me. It wasn't long before we reached a ridge that was laden with huge, gray boulders. Some of the moss covered megaliths were as big as a small house. We meandered our way through the stone giants before reaching the highest point of the ridge. It was there that I saw it. I cringed with fear when standing before us was a rectangular shaped boulder nearly ten feet in height. Several thick vines that hung from a limb high above our head slithered down across the face of the oddly-shaped rock. The huge monolith contained an etching of what appeared to be a hairy man or beast. We felt that it was ancient because the slow effects of erosion had caused the figure to chip and flake. When Willie walked up beside the monolith we heard a loud crunch below the weight of his feet. He kicked aside the decaying leaves and topsoil and uncovered several fragments of what appeared to be pottery. The tiny paintings of fish and animals which adorned the clay pieces revealed that it was likely Native American. "This must be the 'shy-things' front door," Willie declared without a hint of fear as to what may lie ahead. I was a different story altogether. This monument was clearly a warning and I reckoned how angry this thing would be if we trespassed onto its land. I couldn't handle the thought of being ripped to shreds by a ten foot tall, wild man or man-beast or whatever the heck this thing was. "What about my parents," I thought, "would I ever see them again?"

Willie grabbed the pillow case from my hand and started unloading the goods. "This is where we leave the offering," he declared as he leaned the jug of syrup against the base of the huge, stone pillar. He removed the corn-dodgers and placed several of them on the ground next to the syrup. He then twisted open the lid of the berry preserves and dunked one of the remaining corn-dodgers into the jam before cramming it into his mouth. "Want some?" he asked while dipping another biscuit into the fruit jelly. "You better save something for him," I stammered and shivered, referring to the figure etched in the ancient rock. "Willie, aren't you the least bit worried about possibly running into this thing?" I asked while staring up at the ancient artwork. Again, I could envision the gnashing of long, sharp teeth and blood soaked claws while being eaten alive. Yet Willie showed no signs of fear whatsoever. He just shrugged it off and continued to set up a buffet for the 'shy-thing'. I couldn't believe the lack of concern Willie exhibited considering we were miles away from the nearest farm and standing in the heart of the beast's domain.

"Okay! We're good to go," Willie announced, satisfied with the display of sweet things he just set up. "Let's have a sandwich and then find a good place to camp," he proclaimed while reaching into the saddlebag and removing a couple of ham sandwiches.

He downed the sandwich in a matter of minutes and then made short work of the one I had refused. I was too darned frightened to eat. I even suggested that we turn back, that maybe this wasn't such a good idea. But Willie reminded me that we had already come this far, and besides, Walter Tucker's life was at stake. "Quit being a coward!" Willie demanded as he gathered up the pillow case and tossed it over his shoulder. "Okay, but could you please quit being so loud," I said quietly before scanning the surrounding countryside. "We don't need to draw any attention to us," I reasoned.

Willie pushed forward and I reluctantly followed. As we cleared the ridge and neared the summit I stopped to gather myself. Something wasn't right, I thought as I again scanned the surrounding terrain. The greenery was much different and the tall stands of birch and poplar had now given way to hickory, red oak and hazel nut trees.

But it wasn't the abundance of nut trees that drew my attention. It was the lack of wildlife in the area. There was no chattering of squirrels or chirping of chipmunks, and certainly no chorus of songbirds. When I informed Willie about my observation, he did consider it a bit unusual. He then suggested that all the noise I was making by trudging through the leaves was probably spooking everything on the mountain. "Pick-up your feet," he ordered and pushed on. It wasn't long before we reached the large grassy knoll. We skirted along the wood line for a hundred yards or so until Willie found a convenient little clearing to set up camp. A rocky knob provided us with ample stones for a fire pit and a small spring snaked across the flat before plummeting down a steep hillside and crashing into Halyday Run. We spent the next hour clearing the campsite of brush and shrubs. Finally it was time to relax, if that was possible. We had covered nearly five miles and most of it was uphill, therefore not only was I frightened about our isolation, I was also exhausted.

After we settled in, I was somewhat relieved to hear the chatter of chickadees and the cursing of some jaybirds in the distance. Willie spotted a couple of plump, groundhogs feeding out in the meadow. So we were no longer alone, I reassured myself. Eventually my appetite returned and while Willie struggled to start a fire, I woofed down two sandwiches. An hour later dusk arrived, as did the raspy chorus of cicadas and crickets. Willie's fire was now a blazing inferno and I welcomed the strange sense of security it offered. When darkness finally blanketed the mountain, Willie suggested we do some site seeing. " It's dark," I anxiously reminded him. He reminded me that there was a full moon. "Come on, we'll be back in no time," he said as he staggered into the twilight beyond the firelight. "Darn fool!" I hollered as I followed him into the woods. A few hundred yards later we came to the edge of the bluff that overlooked the Allegheny. It was some spectacle as the village we visited on the previous day appeared to be a hundred miles away. Tiny specks of light from the villager's candle lanterns dotted the pitch black landscape and a couple of bonfires blazed in the distance. The river was reflecting the bright moonlight from its transparent surface. It resembled a giant, slithering glass snake.

While awestruck by the beautiful view, a sudden thought came to my head. I couldn't help but feel that Willie had been here before. "How come we didn't get lost trying to find this place?" I asked aloud. Willie's attention was still diverted to the scenery below. "Have you been here before?" I asked him. The boy then removed something from the front pocket of his britches. The metallic object shined in the moonlight when he handed it to me. It was a small, brass compass. "When my Pa was a young man, he was a surveyor for the government. He taught me how to navigate in the woods," Willie claimed before heading back towards our campsite. We unraveled our blankets and stretched them out on the ground near the fire. I nearly forgot about my fear as we laughed and joked over the next hour. When we grew sleepy, Willie announced that he'd take first watch. He then removed a pocket watch from his saddlebag and held it in the light of the fire. "It's ten o'clock. You sleep for a few hours and it'll be your turn to stand watch." A startled look came about my face. "What ?" Willie asked observing my puzzled expression. "Stand watch", I repeated, "What are we supposed to do if that thing arrives in camp?" I asked. Willie just smirked, "Run! Because obviously he didn't have a hankering for your Mother's berry preserves," he snickered. "By the way, she needs to add more sugar to the corn biscuits, because they're a little bland," he laughed some more. "Real funny," I remarked as I nestled up in my blanket and stared into space. I watched as the orange embers from the fire danced high into the night sky before fizzling out and vanishing into the darkness. Eventually my exhaustion got the better of me and sleep finally came.

A light condensation covered my face as I was suddenly awoken by a loud, grumbling noise. I wiped my face with the blanket and rubbed the sleep from my eyes. The gasping fire was still bright enough to light up the surrounding woods. Amongst   illuminated tree trunks I spotted Willie, sound asleep and snoring away. I then peered up into sky and guesstimated that it was two or three o'clock in the morning. With the morning chill settling in, I tossed aside the blanket and made my way to a small pile of kindling wood that Willie had gathered earlier. I tossed a couple pieces onto the choking flames and recovered my blanket before plopping down next to the warmth of the fire. Moments later, above the crackling of the intensifying fire, I thought I heard a ruckus of some sort. Trying to find the origin of the sound I looked back over at Willie, he was still leaning up against the trunk of an ancient pin-oak tree and asleep.

I heard the noise again, only this time it was more pronounced. It sounded like something was moving about woods. I then determined that it was footsteps amongst the clutter of the forest floor. I wrapped the blanket around me tightly and tucked my head into the false sense of security it provided. I was now shivering from both the chill in the air and whatever was moving in the woods. While carefully scanning the surrounding forest I spotted a movement amongst the pulsating light reflecting off the trees. The footsteps grew louder and shadows began darting about the darkness beyond the firelight. I was terrified when I spied the shadow of a large figure amongst the backdrop of the forest. As it was closing in on me, I jumped to my feet and made a mad dash for Willie. I grabbed him by the shoulders and franticly shook him to get him to wake up. "Let's go Willie! Let's go!" I shouted into his ear. Willie rolled his eyes and then pushed me away, before falling back against the tree. " Willie! There's something out there! Wake up!" but it was to no avail. "Let me sleep", he mumbled and started snoring again.

I grabbed the candle lantern from a limb above Willie's head and started for what I figured to be, due East. In sheer panic and reckless abandonment I pummeled through the dark woods. Tree limbs and saplings smacked me in the face and I stumbled over several small boulders as I fought my way down the mountainside. Several minutes later I reached a small flat that I assumed was the base of Hogback. A moment later, the ground beneath my feet gave way and I plummeted thirty or forty feet into a ravine where I landed in a slimy bog covered in peat moss and skunk cabbage. I reeked but fortunately for me, it was a soft landing. I then struggled to free myself from the muck and upon doing so, made another mad dash through the woods. Sore and bruised I eventually made my way down to the creek where I plunged in headfirst. I splashed across the waist deep water until reaching the opposite bank where I paused to catch my breath. When I peered back at what I had left behind, I could barely see the flickering glow of the fire from high atop Hogback. I worried about poor Willie and I prayed aloud that he would be safe. "I've got to get help," I said to myself before recovering my feet and sprinting forward. I ran for awhile until I reached the trail leading back into our valley. I followed it for several hundred yards until I spotted candle light on the hillside above.

As I closed in on the flickering morsel of light, I could make out the outline of Shem Clive's house in the glow of the moonlight. I then reasoned that Clives would help me rescue Willie therefore I shinnied up the crumbling earthy slope and stumbled across the brushy plateau. Before reaching the front porch of the house, Clive's hound started howling. The mangy dog's howl turned into the hoarse bellow of a bark and moments later, I heard the front door crash open. Before I could identify myself, the blast from a shotgun rang in my ears. I dropped to the ground as an ounce of lead birdshot whizzed overhead. While Clives reloaded his musket, I sprung to my feet and headed for the woods beyond his house. "I'll get you yet, you no good varmint!" he hollered while charging his gun. When I reached Clive's barn I was too exhausted to go any farther. Instead of trying for the woods, I staggered into the barn and looked for a place to hide. Bright moonlight filtering through the opened doors illuminated much of the interior. I stumbled over something furry and wrestled with it momentarily before I realized that it wasn't alive. I discovered that it was a buffalo skin robe and tossed the shaggy garment onto the floor. With the sound of approaching footsteps, I desperately searched for a place to hide. Near the stables I found a large grain bin that appeared to be empty. I jumped inside and cringed in pain when several sharp, metallic objects poked me in the backside. I grabbed one of my tormentors and raised it up in the moonlight. It was an iron trap, and just one of many that were causing me discomfort. Upon closer inspection I observed the letters W.T. etched in the jaws of the trap.

Above the squealing of some restless pigs, I could hear the sounds of approaching footsteps. I remained completely still as Clives, with musket in hand, ventured inside the barn. Though I was terrified, I remained completely still. The stocky farmer poked around for a few minutes before exiting the barn. "Darn fox. I'll get you yet!" he shouted aloud before retreating back inside the house. It was now time to make my break. I got up enough energy to climb out of the bin and dash out of the barn. I scattered a flock of chickens before disappearing into a field of standing corn. I busted through rows and rows of the thick stalks before finally reaching the woods. I then fought my way through the dense entanglement of some red brush before I lost my footing and crashed to the ground. I rolled over on my back and gasped for air. I laid there for quite some time while sadly contemplating the fate of my dear friend. The guilt of leaving him behind started to fester in my mind and probably would have consumed me if I hadn't started to grow cold. The ground below my back was smooth like clay, and damp and frigid. In the brilliant moonlight I could see that I was in a tiny clearing nestled right in the center of an acre lot of underbrush. I sat up and wondered why this particular piece of ground wasn't covered in leaves or brush. I noticed something protruding from the muddy surface only a few feet away. At first I reckoned it was some sort of sprout but upon closer inspection, I saw something that made my blood curdle. Three, chalky-colored fingers jetted up from the ground. The middle finger looked as if it had been gnawed by a rodent because much of the flesh and bone was visible. As I recovered my feet, the sky above me opened up and another burst of brilliant moonlight enveloped my trembling frame. And it was then when I realized that I was standing atop a shallow grave. "My god!" I screamed upon the realization of my find. I fought through the remaining brush and high-tailed it into the woods. I ran and ran until I could run no more.

Chapter 11

By dawn I was completely exhausted, both physically and mentally. I sat on the hillside above the trail near Ham McClintock's place, contemplating my next move. Should I return to Hogback for Willie's sake? Or journey home and tell my folks the truth. Though I would receive a good tongue lashing from my Mother, and a whip lashing from my Father, they would know what to do. I was almost certain it was Walter Tucker buried in the mud behind Shem Clive's farm. Why else would Clives have Tucker's traps in his barn? And why was the nervy fool shootin' at me? He couldn't really have mistaken me for a fox. I asked myself over and over again.

As the sun stretched above the hills I worked my way down to the trail and headed back towards the village. I had convinced myself that going back to find Willie was what I needed to do. As I rounded the bend below Glen Barker's property I observed someone approaching in the distance. Concerned that it might be Clives, I left the trail and concealed myself in a giant elderberry bush. Moments later I was relieved to find that it was my friend. Before I could tell Willie about my find, he let me have it. A good stout punch to the abdomen sent me reeling to the ground. I eventually recovered my wind and upon regaining my feet, reminded him that I tried desperately to wake him. With that testimony I could see the anger leave his face. He said I was forgiven and then told me that the campsite was indeed raided by a hairy beast. Willie claimed that three or four ham sandwiches were stolen from his saddlebag. With that revelation I could feel a lump forming in my throat. "So, Chiye-tanka is real," I concluded. Willie smirked, "No silly. The hairy beast was an old raccoon!"

"I think I found Tuck," I told Willie. Before I could say anymore, Willie interrupted, "Good! We can be done with this nonsense. Where is the old squatter?" he asked.

"I think he's buried behind Shem Clives' place." Upon my revelation, Willie just smirked. He thought over his next response. "At first you believed an old Indian myth had abducted Tuck, and then the Half-Breed down at the village drew your suspicion. And now you believe that Shem Clives is the culprit! Who's next?" I then told him about my find. "Are you sure?" He asked with a puzzled look about his face. When I told him about the human fingers sticking up through the ground and about finding the traps, Willie finally believed me.

With some reluctance we went home to tell our folks. It was the right thing to do. My mother nearly had a fit when I arrived home and she saw my torn and bloodied shirt and mud stained britches. I was also covered from head to toe with bruises and abrasions.

My Pa then escorted me over to Jonathon Rynds' farm where they questioned me about my find. "Are you positive?" Mister Rynd asked me again. "Yes, Sir," I answered confidently. My Pa knew I possessed a big imagination, but he also knew that I was usually honest. So when my Pa vouched for me, Mister Rynd agreed that it needed to be investigated..

On the following morning my Pa and Mister Rynd rode to Franklin, to the County Seat. Later that afternoon they arrived back at our farm with two Venango County Deputy Sheriffs where I was interviewed by the lawmen. Their first concern was whether the gravesite was actually on Clive's property. If so, they would have to return to Franklin and obtain a search warrant. I told them that from my best recollection, the site was several yards beyond his property line, in the woods. I didn't believe that Clive's owned those woods. One of the deputies, a strong physical specimen himself, was confident that Clives would cooperate, "Especially if he knows what's good for him!" he concluded.

That evening, the armed Lawmen along with my Pa and Mister Rynd rode over to Clives' Farm. They were warmly greeted by the Farmer. When informed of the reason for their visit, Clives claimed that he had buried some hog remains on the land behind his farm. My Father later revealed that there was a subtle concern about Shem's face when the Deputies asked permission to look the property over. Clives was at first reluctant, but eventually cooperated. When one of the Deputies asked Clives to escort them around his property, he refused claiming that his rheumatism was acting up. The Farmer opted to remain in the house. The stronger of the two Deputies indiscreetly placed his hand on the butt of his Colt Navy revolver and strongly suggested that Clives not leave the house prior to their return. Shem gave them his word that he'd stay put, "Until this nonsense was over", he grumbled.

The men then nosed around Clives' farm for some time before proceeding to the wood line and locating the tiny clearing I had told them about. Sure enough, they saw the same thing I had seen. One of the Deputies returned to Clive's barn and recovered a shovel. The men took turns digging and within minutes exhumed a body from the shallow grave. "Well, the boy was right," one of the Deputies proclaimed while looking over the decomposing corpse. "I think Clives has some explaining to do," he added as they returned to the house to arrest Shem Clives. With guns drawn, the Lawmen went into the house. They spent several minutes searching inside but it was to no avail, Clives was gone. One of the Lawmen noted that the musket that hung above Clive's fireplace was also missing. "He couldn't have gotten far. He's probably headed down to the village to hide out amongst the locals!" the Deputy claimed. "Should we gather a posse?" my Pa asked. The Deputies briefly thought it over. "No. I don't think that will be necessary. He's on the run, but we'll get him before he leaves the County!" the older of the two Deputies claimed confidently.

My Pa and Mister Rynd agreed to remain at Clive's farm until he was captured. The Lawmen were concerned that he might double back. Before their departure one of the Deputies handed my Pa one of his Colt's revolvers. "If he returns, do what you have to. He's a fugitive now," the Lawman said before climbing onto his horse and riding for the village.

CHAPTER 12

The Deputies conducted a thorough search of the village and the surrounding countryside. When they were unable to locate Clives, they called on the assistance of a local tracker and his blood hound. Jeremiah Mitchell's dog had been utilized in the past to locate lost children. Shortly before nightfall the two Deputies, Mitchell and his dog returned to Clives' farm and fetched a piece of the Farmer's clothing. Once the hound got Clive's scent, the tracking began. At nightfall the party had tracked Clive's trail as far as the steep hillside beyond the Clatt Farm. Because it was to dark to go any further, the tracking party found a flat spot below the ridge and set up camp. They would resume tracking at first light.

At around midnight the men finished up the last pot of coffee before designating a watch and turning in. Suddenly a terrible commotion took place in the woods above them. The hound started howling as the

Lawmen reached for their guns. Moments later an object was hurtled through the trees and landed at one of the Deputies feet. It was Shem Clive's musket. The Deputy noticed that the barrel had been bent in two. While at the ready, the men peered out into the darkness beyond the fire light. The wrestling of leaves and the sound of approaching footsteps caused the men to raise their big pistols. "I surrender! Don't shoot! I surrender!" Shem Clives stumbled out into the light of the campfire with his hands raised high above his head. "Please! call off your posse, I don't want no more trouble!" he declared as the Deputies took him into custody. "There ain't no posse, you fool," one of the lawmen informed him. Clives was trembling with fear. "You mean those big men in the dark, on the mountain, weren't yours?" he asked while being cuffed. The Deputies were confused. "Nope! It's just me, Deputy Miller, Mister Mitchell, and his hound. How much have you had to drink?" the Lawmen asked after securing the cuffs.

Clives was escorted to the County Jail where he later confessed to the murder of Walter P. Tucker. He claimed that it was an accident. Apparently Clives had confronted Tucker while he was fishing along Oil Creek. The Farmer was upset because he felt that Tucker wasn't giving him an equal share of the profits made from his Corn Mash Whiskey and Hard Apple Cider. The heated argument turned into a physical confrontation and he hit Tucker in the head with a broken tree limb. Shem claimed that it was in self-defense. Upon receiving the blow, Tucker fell over a steep embankment and crashed facedown on the creek bank. When Clives discovered that the old man was dead, he panicked and drug the body back to his farm where he buried it. Shem Clives was later sentenced to 20 years of hard labor.

Walter Tucker's body was moved to the little cemetery at our Church in Oakland Township. After the funeral, I found myself sitting alone at Tuck's gravesite. When I placed Tuck's tattered old hat on the headstone, tears rolled down across my cheeks. I paid my last respects. My Father came over and gently patted me on the back, attempting to comfort me. I wiped away the tears as we both focused onto Tuck's grave. "Pa. Do you suppose people will think I'm foolish because I believed a 'wild man' got him?" I whimpered. "No Son. I don't think so. I think the people in this valley would rather believe that his death was at the hands of a 'wild man' than from one of their own."

A few days after the funeral, me and Willie Rynd journeyed back to Moody Run.

In a gesture of respect, we tidied up Tucks' shanties and buried the rotting fruit and moldy corn. We then ventured up the rocky hillside above the quiet homestead. It took a little looking around but eventually we found the rocky vault that contained Tucker's treasured heirloom. I removed the pepperbox pistol from the wool sock and handed it to Willie. "You've certainly earned it," I said in appreciation for all of his help in finding the old Trapper. Willie briefly looked the piece over. I could see the tears forming in his eyes. He then handed the shiny gun back to me. " I think he'd rather you to have it", he declared before wiping his forearm across his tear swollen eyes.

It's been 70 years since Walter Tuckers passing and I still have that old pistol. The cherished piece is tucked away in a safe deposit box here in Franklin, PA. Shortly before the turn of the century, I was visited by another dear friend from my childhood. Sam became famous after he penned a couple of popular books. He also changed his name to Mark Twain.

THE END

Suggested Reading

1. Wallace, Paul A.- Indians in Pennsylvania-PA Historical and Museum Co. 2005

2. Trussell, John B.- William Penn, Architect of a Nation-PA Historical Co. 1998

3. Dolson, Hildegrade- The Great Oildorado-Random House, NY- 1959

4. Szalewicz, Steve S.- Oil Moon Over Pithole-1958

5. Steele, Johnny W.- Coal Oil Johnny- His Book-Franklin Pa. Mongs-1902

6. Aites, Richard W. -The Legend of Coal Oil Johnny-IUniverse, NY 2007